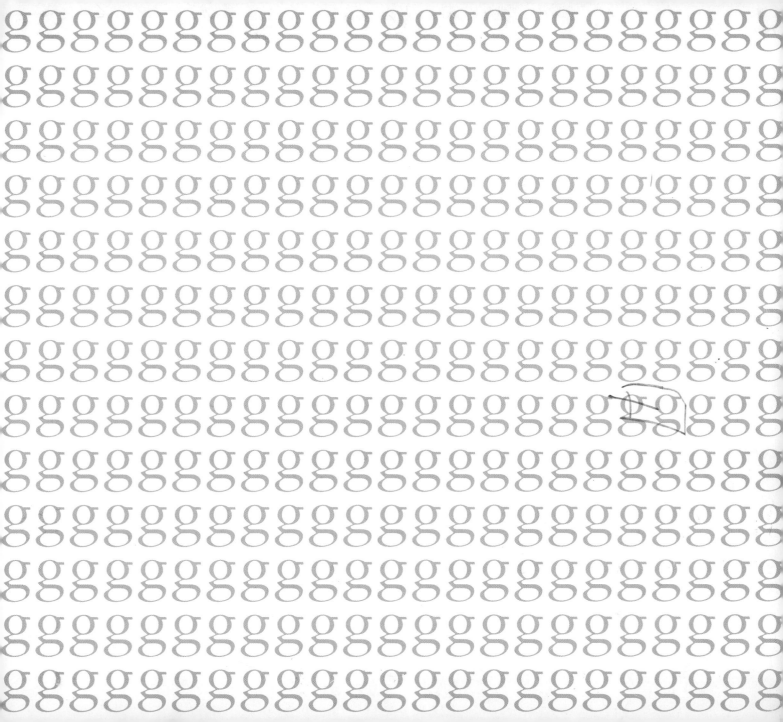

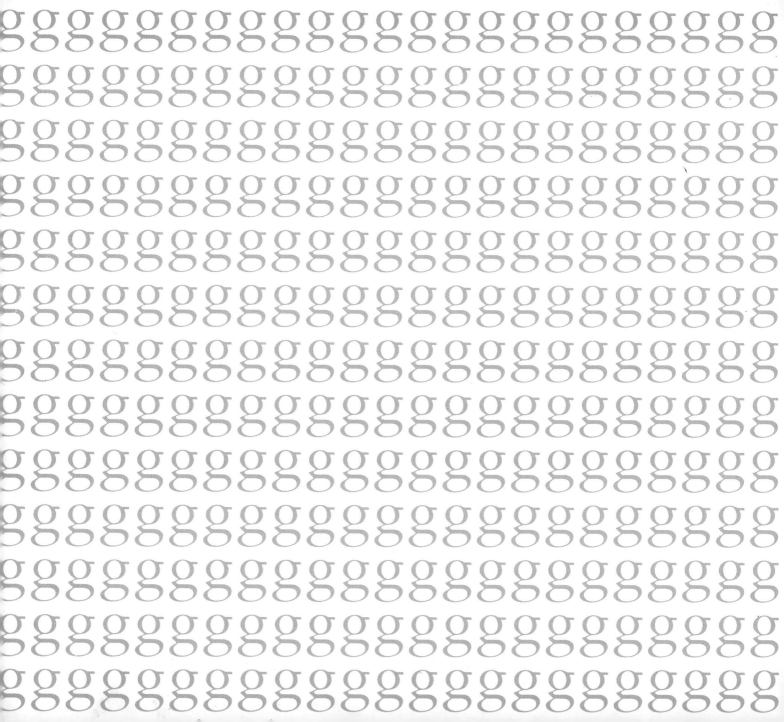

My "g" Sound Box®

(This book uses only the hard "g" sound in the story line. Blends are included. Words beginning with the soft "g" sound are included at the end of the book.)

Library of Congress Cataloging-in-Publication Data
Moncure, Jane Belk.
My "g" sound box / by Jane Belk Moncure; illustrated by Colin King.
p. cm.
Summary: A little girl fills her sound box with many words beginning with the letter "g."
ISBN 1-56766-773-2 (lib. reinforced : alk. paper)
[1. Alphabet.] I. King, Colin, ill. II. Title.
PZ7.M739 Myg 2000
[E]—dc21   99-056561

My "g" Sound Box®

Jane Belk Moncure

illustrated by Colin King

The Child's World®

Little g had a box.

"I will find things that begin
with my 'g' sound," she said.

"I will put them into my sound  box."

Little opened the gate

and went into the garden.

Little g found

goats

in the garden.

Did she put the goats into her box?

She did.

Then Little  found grass,

lots and lots of green grass.

She put the green grass
into the box with the goats.

But the goats ate it all up!

Little  found grapes,

lots and lots of grapes.

She put the grapes into the box.

But the goats ate up all the grapes, too!

What could little  do?

 She found a  gorilla.

She put the gorilla into the box
with the goats.

Did the goats eat the gorilla? No.

The goats grinned.

The gorilla grinned, too.

Little  found a guitar.

She played the guitar.

The gorilla danced.

Then the goats danced with the gorilla.

Everyone giggled!

Little  found some glasses.

She put the glasses on the goats.

Then she found  goggles.

She put the goggles on the gorilla.

Just then, a goose and gander walked by.

"What funny goats! What a funny gorilla!" said the goose and gander.

Little  g caught the goose and gander.

"You belong in my sound box," she said.

The goose got into the box all by herself.
"I will give you a gift," she said.

Then the goose laid an egg made of gold. All of it was made of gold!

Little g looked around her garden.

gate

grapes

guitar

gander

goose

egg of gold

"What a great group of 'g's," she said.

goggles

glasses

glasses

gorilla

goat

goat

grass

Can you read these words

with Little  ?

gum

goldfish

glass

gull

gumdrop

globe

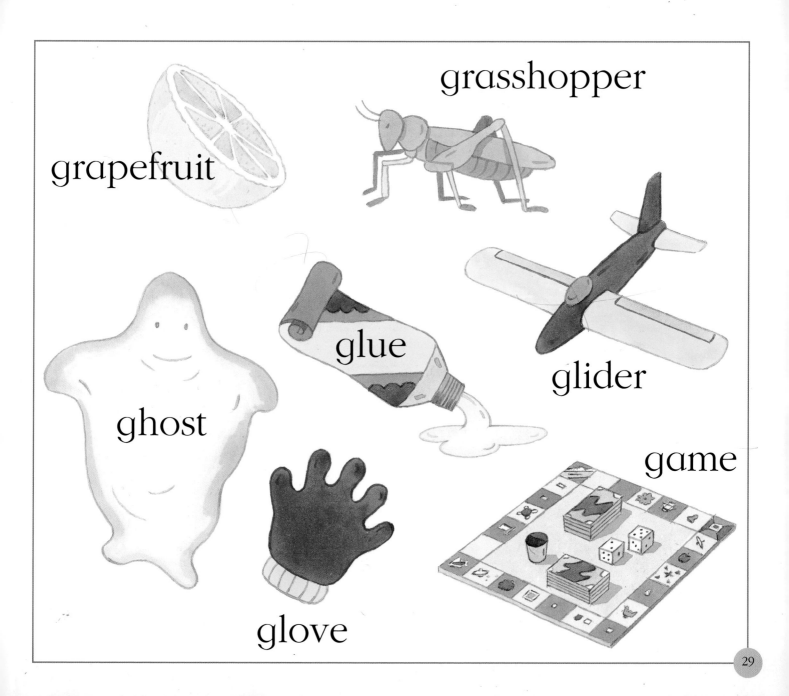

grapefruit

grasshopper

ghost

glue

glider

glove

game

29

In this sound box story, Little g has her own special hard sound.

Little g has another sound, too. It is soft, like the sound of the letter "j."

Can you read these words? Listen for the soft sound.

geranium

giraffe

gingerbread

gerbil

gypsy

ABOUT THE AUTHOR AND ILLUSTRATOR

Jane Belk Moncure began her writing career when she was in kindergarten. She has never stopped writing. Many of her children's stories and poems have been published, to the delight of young readers, including her son Jim, whose childhood experiences found their way into many of her books.

Mrs. Moncure's writing is based upon an active career in early childhood education. A recipient of an M.A. degree from Columbia University, Mrs. Moncure has taught and directed nursery, kindergarten, and primary grade programs in California, New York, Virginia, and North Carolina. As a former member of the faculties of Virginia Commonwealth University and the University of Richmond, she taught prospective teachers in early childhood education.

Mrs. Moncure has travelled extensively abroad, studying early childhood programs in the United Kingdom, The Netherlands, and Switzerland. She was the first president of the Virginia Association for Early Childhood Education and received its award for outstanding service to young children.

A resident of North Carolina, Mrs. Moncure is currently a full-time writer and educational consultant. She is married to Dr. James A. Moncure, former vice president of Elon College.

Colin King studied at the Royal College of Art, London. He started his freelance career as an illustrator, working for magazines and advertising agencies.

He began drawing pictures for children's books in 1976 and has illustrated over sixty titles to date.

Included in a wide variety of subjects are a best-selling children's encyclopedia and books about spies and detectives.

His books have been translated into several languages, including Japanese and Hebrew. He has four grown-up children and lives in Suffolk, England, with his wife, three dogs, and a cat.